Jessie
Christmas 2010
Love you !
Jrh
Nana Riley.

Sharing with You

By Tish Rabe

Illustrated By
Frank Endersby

THOMAS NELSON
Since 1798

NASHVILLE   DALLAS   MEXICO CITY   RIO DE JANEIRO   BEIJING

THE I BELIEVE BUNNY™ SERIES

Sharing with You is the second book in the I Believe Bunny™ Series.

© 2009 by Tish Rabe

The I Believe Bunny™ is a trademark of Tish Rabe.

Published in Nashville, Tennessee, by Thomas Nelson®. Thomas Nelson is a registered trademark of Thomas Nelson, Inc.

Literary agent: Patty Sullivan with p.s. ink publishing solutions

Illustrated by Frank Endersby

Thomas Nelson, Inc., titles may be purchased in bulk for educational, business, fund-raising, or sales promotional use. For information, please e-mail SpecialMarkets@ThomasNelson.com.

Scripture quotations are taken from *International Children's Bible*®. © 1986, 1988, 1999 by Thomas Nelson, Inc. All rights reserved.

Library of Congress Cataloging-in-Publication Data
Rabe, Tish.
Sharing with you / by Tish Rabe ; illustrated by Frank Endersby.
p. cm. — (I Believe Bunny series ; bk. 2)
Summary: Bunny loves to play with Mouse and his other friends, but he does not want to share his collection of shiny rocks with them.
ISBN 978-1-4003-1477-5 (hardcover)
[1. Stories in rhyme. 2. Sharing—Fiction. 3. Rabbits—Fiction. 4. Animals—Fiction.] I. Endersby, Frank, ill. II. Title.
PZ8.3.R1145Sh 2009
[E]—dc22
2009003847

Printed in China

09 10 11 12 MT 6 5 4 3 2 1

Do not forget to do good to others.
And share with them what you have.
These are sacrifices that please God.

HEBREWS 13:16

Once upon a time,
on the first day of spring,
in a flower-filled tree,
a bird started to sing.

Then the I Believe Bunny
said to his friend Little Mouse,
"Come over today and
we'll play at my house."

They played games all morning,
and when they were through,
Mouse said, "I 'd like to share
my favorite flower with you."

Then more friends came by,
Squirrel, Skunk, and Raccoon,
and they all played together
the whole afternoon.

They blew soft dandelions
up into the breeze
and went swinging on vines
hanging down from the trees.

They made pinecone castles and towers of blocks.
Then Mouse said, "Could we play with these shiny rocks?"

Bunny looked at the rocks.
He didn't know what to do.
He knew his friends liked them,
but he liked them too.

These rocks were his favorites.
They gleamed in the sun.
He thought, "I don't want to
share these rocks with anyone."

Then all of a sudden,
Maggie Magpie flew by.
She took one of the rocks
right up into the sky!

"I'll get it!" said Squirrel,
and she started to race.
All the bright butterflies
joined in the chase.

Maggie flew with the rock
to the top of a tree.
"Come back!" Bunny said.
Then Squirrel said, "Follow me!"

"I know Maggie likes
to have bright, shiny things.
I have something to give her
that I found last spring."

"It's a beautiful ring!" said Mouse,
and she was right.
Squirrel showed her friends
how it glowed in the light.

"I can get your rock back,"
said Squirrel. "Soon, you will see."
"Squirrel," Bunny said,
"would you do that for me?"

"You're my friend," said Squirrel.
"And I know one thing;
you mean more to me
than a bright, shiny ring."

They ran back to the tree.
Maggie heard them call.
"Here! Take this ring!"
The rock started to fall!

It bounced off the branches
and flew all around,
then fell in a big pile
of leaves on the ground.

Bunny saw the rock fall
and knew just what to do.
He said, "I have lots of rocks,
and I'll share them with you."

"Let's get back to my house.
This is going to be fun!"
"Okay!" said his friends,
and they started to run.

Just like Mouse with her flower
and Squirrel with her ring,
Bunny knew that sharing
is a very nice thing.

So, each time you share,
you will find, it is true,
sharing is something
God wants us to do.

So, give it a try and
you'll find when you do,
like the I Believe Bunny . . .

you can share too.